KOI'S PYTHON

Miriam Moore
AND Penny Taylor

ILLUSTRATED BY DON TATE

Hyperion Books for Children
NEW YORK

To B. L., who knows and loves
Koi's people as much as I do

—M. M.

To my faithful critics, my
daughters, Natalie and Nacole

—P. T.

Text © 1998 by Miriam Moore and Penny Taylor.

Illustrations © 1998 by Don Tate.

First edition
1 3 5 7 9 10 8 6 4 2

Library of Congress Cataloging-in-Publication Data

The artwork for this book was prepared with gouache and pen and ink.
The text for this book is set in 13-point Leawood Book.

Moore, Miriam,
Koi's python / Miriam Moore ; Illustrated by Penny Taylor.
p.   cm.
Summary: Eleven-year-old Koi is eager to kill a python as part of the rite of
passage to manhood among his Batetela people, but in the meantime
he must face a bully who is picking on an old hunter in the village
marketplace.
ISBN: 0-7868-1227-3 — ISBN: 0-7868-2285-6 (lib. bdg.)
1. Mongo (African poeple)—Juvenile fiction. [1. Mongo (African
people)—Fiction. 2. Pythons—Fiction. 3. Bullies—Fiction.
4. Old age—Fiction.] I. Taylor , Penny , ill. II. Title.
PZ7.M7874Ko   1998
[Fic}—dc21   97-23994

CONTENTS

CHAPTER ONE THE GREAT SNAKE HUNTER 1

CHAPTER TWO KOI THE YAM BOY 9

CHAPTER THREE MADMAN SANKURU 17

CHAPTER FOUR THE MYSTERY SOLVED? 22

CHAPTER FIVE THE BIG FIGHT 29

CHAPTER SIX PYTHON! 38

CHAPTER SEVEN JA-RUN-PA 45

CHAPTER ONE

THE GREAT SNAKE HUNTER

Watch out, python," Koi called as he ran through the jungle to dig the new yam crop. "The mighty Koi is coming. He will claim your skin."

Koi ducked under a vine. He then jumped

in midair, slashing it with his knife. "Take that . . . and that . . . and *that*!"

He looked at the shreds of vine lying at his feet. When would that be a real python he wondered? *His* python!

He leaned against a baobab tree. His best friend, Okale, already had his own python skin. Even that jackal Membele had *his* python skin.

And Koi? Koi looked at the knife in his hand. Koi just had this cutlass. And it had never tasted the flesh of the powerful python.

He kicked the tree in disgust. Would his python never come? Or was he to stay a boy of the Batetela tribe forever?

Suddenly he crouched. Overhead a weaver bird sang. But it trilled up at the end. "Okale?" Koi called into the jungle.

There was silence.

Koi's grip tightened on his knife. He knew his best friend's love of tricks. Okale loved to spring on him from the shadows.

"Faster than a swamp leopard," Okale loved to say about his stealth.

"Mine!"

Koi's arms were pinned to his side. He was caught in a death squeeze. "Stop it, Okale!"

Laughing, Koi began to rock from side to side.

"Sorry, great python hunter," Okale shouted. He braced his feet against the tree. "You are bat dung now!"

Bat dung, huh? With a war cry, Koi jolted forward. He hurled Okale over his head and onto the matted ground.

Grinning, Okale looked up at Koi.

"Ja-run-pa!" Koi began to chant, arms high in victory.

Okale sat up. "Save your victory dance, Koi, for your real enemy, though I can always show you how it's done." There was a challenge in Okale's wide grin.

Koi's arms dropped. "Go ahead, Okale. Remind me I'll never see my python till you and Membele are old men."

4

Okale got up. He stopped grinning. "Ah, Koi, this is their crawling season. I bet your snake is just a shadow away."

He knew his friend was trying to cheer him. But Koi didn't want to feel better. He didn't want anything but to lay eyes on his python of manhood.

"Want to spear some fish?"

Koi shook his head.

"How about digging some manioc root? Papa sent me out here for it."

Okale's father was one of the tribe's witch doctors. He always needed the herbs and wild grasses of the jungle for healing potions.

"Show me again, Okale," Koi insisted, "how you conquered your python."

Okale sighed. How many times would he have to repeat this for Koi?

He began to stage the moment he came upon his python. He had been running under a mahogany tree when he spied the huge snake above his head. It was coiled around a limb. Only its wide head dangled below, waiting.

"So close was he . . .," Okale said.

"I know, I know," Koi interrupted. "So close you felt his hot breath on your shoulder."

"So I jumped back. I grabbed my knife and began to move from side to side."

"To confuse him," Koi continued. "And to give you time to find the best strike point."

Okale nodded. Koi had listened well those many times he had repeated his victory. "And there the strike point was—just below his jaw." Okale grunted as he made a series of thrusts into the air. "Again and again," he added.

Koi felt himself making those same thrusts. His lips were drawn tight.

"So want to see it again?" Okale asked. "The skin is completely dry now."

"Wha—? Oh, no." Koi got to his feet. "I've got to dig yams." To see the skin of Okale's python would only make him sadder.

"Come with me tomorrow to market. Please?"

Okale shook his head. "Papa needs me."

"But you need a new blade for your sickle. You said so yourself. We could then talk more about pythons."

Okale shrugged, "Sorry. *Kutshikali la ki.*"

"*Kutshu la wolu,*" answered Koi as he turned to trudge toward the fields. Okale had said the traditional Batetelan good-bye, which meant "remain in peace." But what "peace" could he have without his python to conquer?

"Koi?"

"Yes?"

"Watch out for Membele. Now that his uncle is on the village counsel, Membele is puffed up like a bellyful of millet."

"Forget Membele," Koi answered firmly. "That's one snake that stalks his own tail."

Okale laughed. "See you after market. Then how about some frog trappings?"

They loved to chase frogs. No Batetelan

ever touched a frog. They were taboo. One touch and one was cursed for life. But nobody said you couldn't tease them!

Koi waved his answer. Mama would wonder if he were late from the fields. After all, she needed him to check each yam. Ever since his papa had gone to the city to find work, Mama's market yams were what kept them fed.

CHAPTER TWO

KOI THE YAM BOY

"T est every step, *Onami*," Koi's mother called from the door of the hut.

Koi waved as he headed down the jungle path. She was really telling him to watch out for any lurking python. After all, the mighty serpent was the master of tricks and could move at the speed of an arrow, stretching over its prey faster than the "Hand of Death." At least, that's what Okale's papa often said. So Koi knew how she worried about that moment when he would meet the great rock python.

Koi worried about it, too. But he would never let his mother know. After all, she had lost a young brother to his manhood python. It was something she used to talk about. But not anymore. Not since Koi turned eleven.

Walking along the narrow path, he began to make slashing motions with his knife. "Ja-run-pa! Ja-run-pa!" He loved making the fierce sounds of a mighty Batetelan hunter. "Ja-run-pa!" He thrust at the imaginary python. Now it hung from a cottonwood tree, now from a mango tree. He knew all the python's usual attack positions—from a limb, hiding against a log, even playing dead. But of course there was the great mystery move. How could he know that? This was only shared by father with son. It could never be repeated from boy to boy. That was a tribal taboo.

The thought made Koi kick at a stone. Well, that was one move he would just have to learn some other way. His papa had been in the city almost two years now. He always sent money. But what about the secret he owed him?

"Watch out, you slithering one," Koi called again. "Koi the fearless hunter is ready for your tricks."

THR-UMPF!

Koi jumped, jabbing at the air.

But it was only the sack of yams on his back. The orange yams were rolling every-where. Embarrassed, he snatched up his mother's vegetables. Morning market was already bustling in the village.

Koi loved the market. There was the rich aroma of roasted coconut. It came from the old woman's cart. She was always patting coconut slices into millet cakes. "Moyo,

Koi," she greeted. "Your mama on her feet?"

"Moyo!" he answered. "In the garden before sunrise."

"Good," the old woman nodded. "And now she has a tall son to help her?"

Koi tried to smile. He knew he wasn't tall, not like the other boys.

The next stall sold millet pudding. The young sisters sang a chant. They always used the onlooker's name in their song.

> Here is Koi with a sack.
> Our millet pudding will bring him back.

A few coins would buy the porridge. But Koi's coins were to buy a new cutlass, not pudding. He needed a new knife to trim the market yams. So he shook his head and looked down.

But all the wonderful aromas were free.

"Koi," one of the sisters whispered. "Better hurry your mama's yams to the stall."

"Why? Is he mad?" The sun showed he

wasn't late. Besides, the man who bought the yams was always friendly.

"No," she whispered. "It's . . . it's just better if you get to the south side quickly."

Koi thanked her and began to run. What was going on?

"Hey, yam boy!"

Koi cringed. Now he understood her warning. But he didn't turn. He knew too well it was that jackal Membele.

"Koi the yam boy!" Membele shouted. "Where's your mighty python? In your pocket?"

Koi tried to ignore him as he hurried past the stalls. Ever since Membele had moved into the village to live with his rich uncle, he always taunted Koi. He especially taunted him about bringing his mother's yams to market. Membele seemed to forget those years he worked in the fields, too. Sometimes he would even snap his fingers and point.

Koi just wanted Membele to go away. Especially when he heard that snapping

sound. He hated Membele's finger snapping worst of all. It made the other village
boys begin to snap their fingers louder and
louder.

Sometimes Koi felt like the whole market
was staring at him. The snapping seemed
to grow as loud as cicadas in the night
grasses. Then Koi wanted to just throw
down the sack of yams and run back into
the jungle.

"What's in your sack?" Membele laughed.
"Baby pythons? They won't make you a
man. A victory python has to be as tall as a
warrior, remember?" He snickered. "But
what would you know about warriors?"

Koi turned away. He couldn't believe that
he and Membele once harvested millet
together. He had been almost nice then.
They even drank from the same gourd. Of
course, that was before the brushfire that
killed Membele's family. But ever since he
moved in with his rich village uncle,
Membele had acted like a puffing adder. At

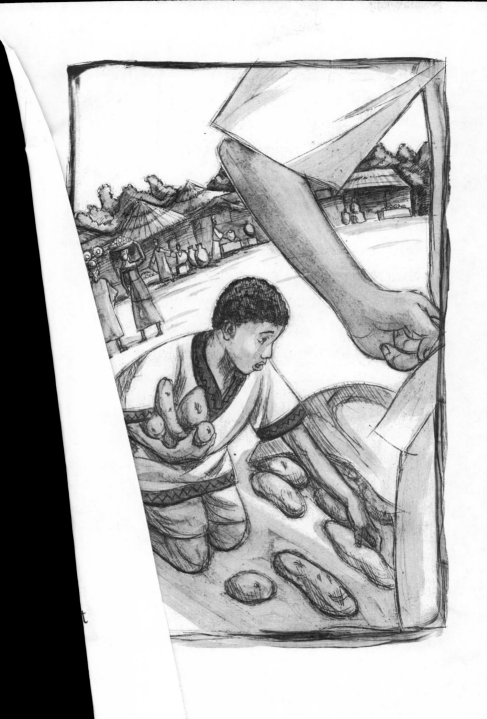

least he acted that way with his old friends from the brush.

THR-UMPF!

Koi clenched his teeth. He felt the yam sack growing lighter. Oh, no, not again! Hurriedly he squatted down. He began to gather them again in his arms.

"Oh, poor Koi the yam boy. He's traded pythons for Mama's vegetables."

He felt Membele's shadow over him.

"Yam boy! Yam boy!" The voices were those of Membele's friends. "Mama's yam boy!"

Koi tried to shut it out. He tried to think of the mighty python he would conquer someday. Then he would no longer be Koi the yam boy. He would be a man—a Batetelan man.

But suddenly Koi heard another sound, a bursting sound, above him.

"Ja-run-pa!"

Koi's toes dug into the dust. His heart lurched. That could only be one person!

16

CHAPTER THREE

MADMAN SANKURU

Koi squinted up. He saw Sankuru, the old man who lived under the mango tree. Everyone called him Madman Sankuru. Half-dancing, half-crouching, he was thrashing his familiar stick about. Yet he was creeping slowly toward Membele and his friends.

His strange yellow eyes were usually rolling and wild. But now they were steady and pinned on Membele. Sankuru stared at Membele as though the boy was a swamp leopard and he was a mighty hunter ready for the kill.

"Away, Sankuru!" Membele shouted. He slapped at the old hunter's stick. "Go crawl under your mango tree."

But Sankuru only paused. He clutched his stick weapon in both hands and raised it slowly over his head.

"Look out!" shouted one of the boys.

Sankuru was aiming at Membele's head.

"Madman!" Membele shouted as he leaped sideways. He grabbed the old man's stick and began to break it on his knee.

Sankuru lost his look of fierce concentration and only looked confused.

"Don't!" shouted Koi. "Don't break his weapon!"

A sly smile crawled across Membele's broad face. He threw the stick up in

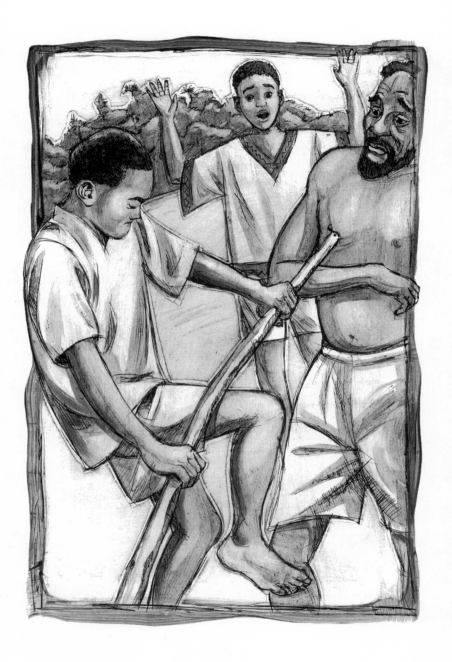

the mango tree. It hung on a limb.

"Madman Sankuru who hunts with sticks," the boys shouted as they dashed into the throng that had gathered. "What's your kill, Madman? Bedbugs?" Membele looked at Koi. "Or is it little boys with yam sacks?"

Their laughter hung in the air like the stench of rotting flesh. Koi looked into the yellow eyes of the old one.

"Please," Koi said as he jumped to retrieve the man's stick. "Please don't try to help me." He grabbed the stick and handed it to Sankuru.

The old warrior reached for his stick, but his hand was trembling.

"I'm not afraid of Membele and his gang. Truly I'm not," Koi tried to tell him.

But it was no use.

"Ja-run-pa!" The old man began to whomp the ground.

"Ja-run-pa!" He began to slash the air.

"Ja-run-pa!" He began to slice the air sideways.

Despite his worries, Koi felt the old one's energy wash over him. What a warrior he must have been, Koi thought as he slipped toward the yam vendor. I bet he knows everything about the deadly python!

But his thoughts were interrupted. He could hear Membele and his gang laughing at Sankuru's "dance." Koi looked around desperately at the market women. They could usually calm the old one.

"Sankuru?" the coconut woman called.

Koi sighed deeply. *At last*, he breathed.

It was a mother's voice. "It is still warm."

Koi tightened his grip. Already he hated the thought of market tomorrow—Membele would never let him alone now that he had stood up for Madman Sankuru.

CHAPTER FOUR

THE MYSTERY SOLVED?

Y ou could be hyena meat," Okale said glumly. He was chasing a frog toward a stream. "You know better than to cross Membele. And in front of his new village friends?"

Koi didn't answer. He was too busy zigzagging in front of their trapped frog. He loved this game. Although he ran the risk of being touched, it still gave him good practice for bigger prey—like a python.

"Ah, Okale, I'm not afraid of Membele. We used to drink from the same field gourd, remember?"

Okale grabbed a twig and stripped it. "Well, he may have another cup for you tomorrow—a bitter one."

Koi took a piece of bark and flipped the spotted frog into the stream.

"Good work!" Okale shouted. He began a victory dance. "Again the cursed frog is untouched."

Koi squatted by a bush. He didn't feel like any victory dance. He couldn't get old Sankuru off his mind. He could still feel the surge of energy from his wrinkled body.

"Okale?"

"Hmmm?" He was looking up at a eucalyptus tree for another frog.

"You know that old man Sankuru?"

"The one who lives under the mango

tree?" Okale was slapping at the trunk. "The one who once hit the tribal leader with his stick?"

Koi sat forward. "He did?" He laughed out loud. "Why?"

"The leader tried to have him tied in a wagon and hauled over to the mission station. But the old one whacked him on the head. It made the leader so mad—right there for the whole market to see—that he slapped his leg, turned, and walked away."

Koi nodded. To slap one's leg was to declare one an enemy.

Okale sighed. "The brains of a crazy man are like gourd seeds—loose and rattly."

Koi sprang to his feet. He grabbed Okale and began to shake his friend's head. "Like this?"

Both boys hit the ground, tumbling over and over, laughing and coughing.

That evening, Koi sat by the fire. He watched his mother pounding yams.

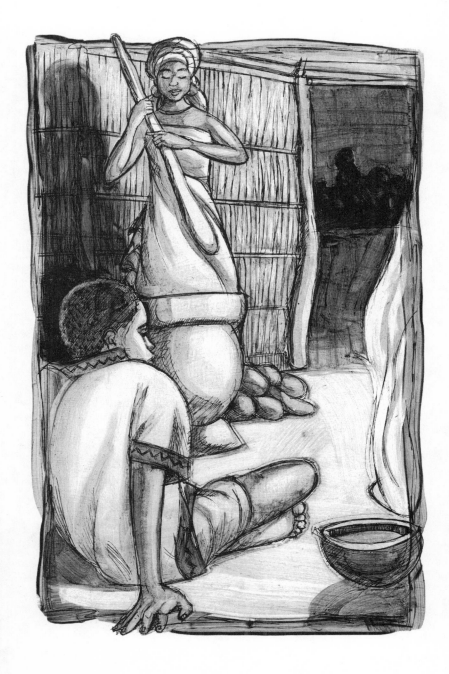

"Why do people taunt the one called Sankuru?"

"Because he lived a life they can never have," she replied softly.

"I don't understand."

"Now our people farm more than hunt." She explained that Sankuru was once a great Batetelan hunter. "That's when the leopards were as numerous as cicadas."

She sat back on her heels. "There was a time when Sankuru alone could feed a whole village." She turned to Koi. "And from just one hunt. I was just off my mother's back, but I remember those times." She dropped yam cakes in the hot oil. "Once every young Batetelan wanted to be like Sankuru—tall, fearless, with hands as steady as baobab trunks."

Koi remembered the way the stick had trembled in Sankuru's hands. "But why does he act that way?"

"He is old, son."

"No, I mean," he paused. "You know,

like he's always on a hunt."

His mother smiled. "Maybe he is. Maybe he has retreated to the world he knows best."

"But—"

"Remember the brushfire that took away many of our neighbors? Membele's parents, for instance."

Koi's stomach tightened.

"Well, Sankuru's family was also taken. Not by a wildfire—a fever. His wife and his children in one week's time." She sat back and stared into the bubbling palm oil. "That's why he lives in his own world and sleeps outside under the mango tree."

She then said something else. But Koi was not listening. He was trying to imagine the old man as a young mighty warrior. He could see the people running out to claim a portion of his kill.

"Mama?"

"Humm?"

"Did he ever hunt pythons? I mean as a

man, not just to prove himself."

Her smile faded. "Sankuru the hunter knew the rhythm of every creature, including the dreaded python."

That night Koi could barely lay on his mat. He knew he had to talk to Sankuru. Perhaps he could tell him about the mystery move of the python. After all, he had spent his life tracking such creatures.

But could he make Sankuru understand? And what about Membele and his gang? Would they leave them alone long enough? He rolled over, listening to the night creatures in the grasses. Slowly his thoughts gave way to slithering pythons. But they had yellow eyes. And weaver birds overhead called out, "Koi-the-yam-boy . . . Koi-the-yam-boy." Soon his mind was stalking other paths, other forests beyond the swamps.

CHAPTER FIVE

THE BIG FIGHT

T hanks for walking with me," Koi said as they neared the village.

"I just wish I could go in with you," Okale said. "Today may not be easy with him. He does not like to forget."

Okale did not have to say the name. Koi knew he meant Membele. He had thought about that, too. All night, in fact. As long as he could remember, no one had ever stood up to that hulk Membele. Especially not now that he lived in his uncle's powerful household.

"But today could turn out more important than that millet-belly," Koi said. He hoped he sounded convincing.

Okale shrugged. "Could be. Could be not. It depends if he leaves you two alone long enough."

Koi shifted the heavy sack to his head. This way he felt as tall as Okale.

Okale turned back toward the fields. "Keep your eyes roaming," he warned. "Remember, Membele is as cunning as a leopard. And nobody would ever touch him. His uncle would see to that."

Koi waved good-bye and hurried toward the market. He didn't want to hear any more.

Nodding to the coconut woman, he hurried past the stalls. There was no sign of

Sankuru. Where was he? Had Membele pulled some trick overnight?

Then he saw something move under the mango. It was Sankuru! He was just now sitting up on his mat.

Koi looked around. Then he ambled over sideways. "Sankuru?"

The old one looked up.

"My . . . my mama sent these." He reached in his pocket and brought out some *leki* cakes.

Sankuru just stared at them.

"She says you fed her family many times. From your hunts."

Sankuru took them hesitantly. One cake fell.

Koi knelt down quickly and picked it up. He slid onto the mango root next to Sankuru's mat. He watched as the old man ate the melon seed oil cakes.

"Sankuru, I am eleven years old. I will face my python soon. I . . . I think I'm ready. But Papa hasn't been home in two years.

So I have no man to teach me."

Sankuru just studied the last cake in his hand.

Koi was disappointed. After a while, he asked, "Did you conquer many rock pythons?"

The old man swallowed the last cake in one gulp. Then he reached for his stick.

Koi's heart thumped. *Oh, please, not the strange stalking dance!*

But Sankuru did not begin his dance. Instead he curled a gnarled finger around the stick. His finger was motionless. He looked at Koi.

Koi looked puzzled.

Then the old man moved the stick slightly. Suddenly his finger tightened around the wood. He moved the stick again, and his finger now squeezed the wooden rod till his knuckle paled.

Koi watched, dumbfounded. What did this mean?

Then the old warrior drew a breath and

held it. His yellow eyes cut to Koi.

Then it hit Koi. *Yes!* Koi jumped to his feet. The python's gauging of breath! He remembered once overhearing some men at the well. They were talking about the many tricks of the rock python. They said once a python is on you, he gauges your fear by your breaths.

"The more breaths, the more he squeezes," one man said. "So your only chance is to hold your breath till the one big strike." The man then paused. "That is, if your lungs survive."

"Yes!" shouted Koi, then caught himself. "That's got to be the mystery move—gauging all breath!" He patted Sankuru's arm. "Thanks, Sankuru. I mean it."

"For what?" came a voice behind him. Koi turned to see Membele and his gang. "For sharing his bedbugs with the mighty python hunter, Koi?" The marketplace echoed with their coarse laughs.

As usual, Koi turned away. Let them

laugh, he told himself. I now know the mystery move. He tried to disappear into the crowd. Sankuru will be safer, Koi thought, if I'm not around.

But suddenly Sankuru was on his feet, stick in hand. With one thrust he slapped Membele, hurling him into the dirt.

But Membele rolled sideways and picked up a stone. It was the size of a young melon. With one spring he was on his feet, starting to circle Sankuru slowly.

"No!" Koi shouted. "You could kill him." Desperately he looked around for any village official. But all had disappeared. Afraid of Membele's uncle, Koi decided quickly.

He tried to meet the gaze of some men. But they turned away. They looked ashamed, but it was obvious they would not risk the hatred of Membele's uncle to save someone called Madman.

Membele was now drawing closer as Sankuru stood there. The old man's knees became wobbly.

Membele's friends were cheering him on.

Membele was now stepping directly toward the old hunter. The boulder was raised above his head.

"No!" Koi shouted. "I mean it, Membele!" And with that he grabbed his yam sack and dumped it at the stalker's feet.

The ground was now alive with yams rolling everywhere. Membele made a kicking motion to clear the path but lost his balance. He landed in a sea of yams—SPLAT! The boulder smashed even more as it rolled away.

All at once the village boys were silent. Membele jerked to his feet.

Koi had never seen Membele so mad. Even his eyebrows twitched.

Some men behind him began to point and laugh. Membele twisted around to see what was so funny.

"It's you, Membele," one man said. "Maybe you need to change your pants."

And with that everyone saw the seat of his pants caked with ripe, smashed fruit. "Our Batetelan hunter who has soiled his pants!" Everyone laughed, even some of the boys.

Membele cut his eyes at Koi. He then spat in the dust and rubbed it out angrily with his sandal.

Koi's heart quickened. He was in deep trouble now. But he looked over at Sankuru, who actually seemed to be smiling. Koi picked up his empty sack.

Well, at least it wasn't the old hunter's head that was smashed, he thought as he slowly walked back to the jungle path. Now if I can just convince Mama we can survive without today's market sale.

CHAPTER SIX

PYTHON!

Long days passed. The dry season lingered. Koi's daily trips to market became even more dangerous. Still, not one python had been spied. But scorpions and spitting adders were now lurking along every path. So his mother insisted he carry a staff.

"But, Mama, I have my knife."

"You need a stick to test your path. Scorpions hide everywhere."

Koi swallowed his breath. To argue with his *nyomi* was to argue with the wind. So he now carried two objects he hated: the staff that looked too much like Sankuru's weapon stick and a sack of yams that had become a punching bag for Membele and his gang.

Ever since Koi took up for the old hunter, Membele and his gang seemed to lie in wait for him these mornings. Sometimes they would jostle the sack on his back; other times they would grab yams and toss them back and forth.

And Membele and his friends pestered Sankuru even worse. They grabbed at his stick or threw rocks. Once they even dumped grubworms on his sleeping mat and stomped on them.

The old hunter would yell at them, then run to the well and crouch there, mumbling. But, as usual, the village men looked the other way.

So Koi grew to hate the market. What was he thinking when he had tripped Membele? He had just made the old one's life more miserable.

But Koi did manage to bring him food. Some came from his mama's pot and some slipped from his own bowl. He would leave it under his tree and watch as Sankuru would check for it each morning.

Still, what Koi could not change, he tried to avoid. Now he got to market before sunrise, delivering the yams and Sankuru's food before Membele was even out of his uncle's house.

Early one morning Koi rushed down the shadowy path. He was thinking about his papa's letter that had arrived the evening before. It said he had gotten a new job.

But he stopped. *What is that? A scorpion!* It backed up, its tail vibrating.

Koi touched his knife.

Suddenly the creature lunged at his foot. *THERE!* Koi flung his knife.

But it glanced off a rock. The scorpion scurried under a bush.

"You just wait!" Koi traced his knife to the roots of a breadfruit tree. He bent over to grab it.

WHUMP! Something hit his back, its weight sending him sprawling.

He felt a cold, slithery touch.

PYTHON! His blood stopped. *I'm trapped under a python!*

But he willed his mind to obedience. He felt the mighty python testing him with slight body spasms.

Sankuru's yellow-eyed gaze crossed his thoughts. *Calm*, he ordered his muscles, *calm. Don't breathe until you are ready to strike!*

The words "faster than the hand of death" rang in his head.

Then he felt the knife pushing against his pinned stomach.

He felt the monster snake insinuate up toward his neck. He even began to smell its acrid breath.

Slowly, slowly, he edged his right hand toward his stomach to grasp the knife. His lungs were now screaming for air.

Soon . . . soon, he tried to tell them. His skin tingled as he felt the snake's sharp head now nudging against his jaw. He gripped the knife tighter.

NOW! And with the surge of jungle lightning, he rolled over, gripping the huge head with his left hand.

The python tightened around his body, cutting his new breath.

But Koi's knife found the soft spot under the jaw. Again and again he jabbed, gasping for air. And with each thrust his body braced for the bone-crushing squeeze of the struggling serpent.

There! Koi felt at last the power slowly flow from his attacker. But he just lay there, heaving for air.

I did it! shouted in his brain. *I really did it, thanks to Sankuru!*

Slowly he crawled to his knees. For the

first time he looked over at his attacker.

His heart thudded. It was as long as a river!

But he felt strangely calm. In fact, he felt like he could conquer anything that came across his path now.

CHAPTER SEVEN

JA-RUN-PA

A thought suddenly curled around his mind. He glanced at the sun. Yes, it was still early.

He struggled to lift the body of the long snake with his staff. Good, he thought. This will work, once balanced. At last he struggled down the narrow path. Ja-run-pa!

throbbed in his ears. Ja-run-pa!

By the time he got to the square, his arms were aching. His chest was heaving so loudly he was afraid the market women would hear him. But they were busy building their fires. Quickly he cut behind the well. This was a shortcut to the mango tree.

In a matter of minutes, Koi was back again. He strolled by the stalls with their roasting coconuts and thick puddings. Again he breathed deeply the rich aromas as he ambled toward the yam vendors.

But just as he passed the vendor of peppers, suddenly there was a shout. "Hey, Sankuru, what's this?"

It was followed by another. Then another. The shouts came from the well.

Koi hid a smile. He ran across the open square. A crowd was gathering around the mango tree. Membele's uncle was even in the front. There stood Sankuru—he was staring at a long snake lying in the dust.

The old man looked confused, but people were nodding deeply.

"Hey, your blood's still warm, old one," one man said as he circled the twisted serpent slowly. "You haven't lost your eye, Sankuru. And this one is a king of rock pythons."

About that time Membele ran up. At first he could not see for the crowd. Then someone told him Sankuru had killed a large python last night. "He's still protecting his people," his uncle said as he scanned the crowd, "a living model for our young men. So from this day on, our Sankuru is to be honored as the hero he is."

A shout of male voices went up in agreement.

Membele's face stretched into a sneer.

But at that moment someone lifted the lifeless snake and draped it on a mango limb in honor of Sankuru's bravery.

Cheers and clapping went up all over the square. The cheers prompted Sankuru to raise his arms in victory. It was like a reflex.

Membele's sneer disappeared.

Koi ran back to the coconut woman and hurriedly eased a coin from his belt. "I want the biggest millet cake you have." He pointed to one frying in the back. "It is for Sankuru the mighty Batetelan hunter."

She smiled and nodded. But she handed him two cakes, not one.

"I only want one." He showed her the coin again.

"One is for Sankuru the mighty Batetelan hunter and one is for the Batetelan boy who is now a man!"

Koi looked at the woman. "You know?"

"I live near your path, remember?" She turned back to her fire. "Carrying snakes through the jungle is very hard work, even harder than yam sacks."

He smiled.

"And Koi?"

"Yes?"

"There will be another victory cake when you bring your *next* python."

Koi nodded to the old woman, took a few steps backward, turned, then ran back to the mango tree. Everyone was cheering as Sankuru began to move through his hunter-dance.

"Ja-run-pa!" He slashed the air.

"Ja-run-pa!" He whomped the ground.

"Ja-run-pa!" He sliced the air sideways.

Koi smiled as he held Sankuru's victory cake. There would be time enough to eat once the old man returned from his triumphant mystical hunt.

"Ja-run-pa!"

But all at once Membele's uncle bellowed, "Membele, you and that market boy," he pointed straight at Koi, "go cut a fitting staff for our Sankuru." He motioned to a grove nearby. "One that befits our brave warrior here."

Membele looked like he had just bitten into a bitter seed. But he cut his eyes over to Koi. "Yeah, market boy," he jeered.

Koi felt his spirits drop to his toes. Why

me? Why now? But he begrudgingly followed his tormentor.

Down at the grove Membele began to climb the tallest tree. "Wait down there, market boy. The greenest limbs are always near the top." He quickly disappeared into the heavy foliage above.

Koi gladly waited on the ground. Why did the uncle have to ruin everything? He was enjoying Sankuru's victory dance, then to be interrupted by—

"AIIEEE! Help!" The cries were so loud the leaves rustled.

"Membele?" Koi squinted up into the green maze. Then like a boulder tumbling down a ravine, Membele's body fell crashing and twisting.

"Get him off me!" Membele's hands were pulling at something wrapped around his shoulders. "Help me, Koi!"

PYTHON! It was glistening silver and as long as a well rope.

"Koi!" Membele's voice was pleading

now as he ricocheted off a limb.

A cut limb crashed at Koi's feet with Membele's knife embedded in it.

THRUMP! Membele and his attacker finally hit the ground, sending up a cloud of dust.

Koi grabbed his own knife as he ran to Membele's writhing body. He had landed on his side, the snake's head angling toward his throat. Membele's arms were flaying desperately to free themselves from the serpent's grip.

"Koi!" The screams echoed up the slope.

Quickly Koi fell to his knees and slid his hand under the python's jaw. Its cool damp skin sent shivers up his arm. He strained to pull its massive head back as he angled his knife. There. Again and again his blade found its mark.

Slowly, too slowly, the snake grew limp in his hand.

Koi sat back on his heels, gasping. He surveyed the long python curled in the

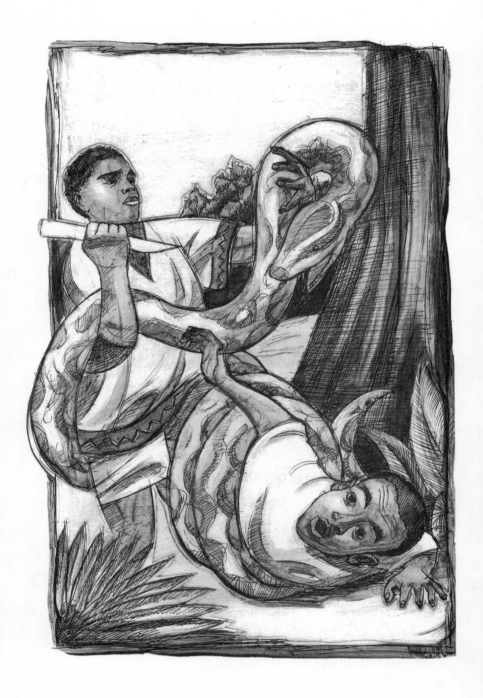

dust. But his heart was thudding too loudly for him to think.

All he could do was stare.

Membele, too, still lay on his side, heaving for breath. But his eyes refused to meet Koi's.

"Hey!" a shout came from behind. "Come look at what the market boy did!" This was followed by the sounds of many footsteps.

Suddenly Koi felt slaps on his shoulders, and his knife was held up for all to see. This brought shouts of praise.

"Come see, Sankuru," someone called as Koi was hoisted high on two men's shoulders. "Your bravery is even spreading to our young warriors. This young man's not only conquered his manhood python, but even saved Membele's life."

"His name is Koi," a feminine voice corrected. It came from the woman who sold cakes. "Koi who has now proven worthy to be a Batetelan man." She smiled up at Koi.

This brought a whoop of male voices as

they carried Koi up the slope like a mighty warrior returning home triumphant.

At the mango tree Sankuru waited with warmth in his yellow eyes.

"Membele," his uncle yelled down the slope to where Membele was getting to his feet. "Get up and bring Koi's python up here. It's a prize that deserves to hang with Sankuru's. We'll display it to inspire our other young men, right, Koi?"

Koi wanted to answer, but he couldn't. All he could do was nod because words, mango-sweet words, were throbbing in his ears.

My manhood python. Ja-run-pa.

Membele, a servant to my python. Ja-run-pa. Ja-run-pa.

Koi, now a Batetelan man among men. Ja-run-pa. Ja-run-pa. Ja-run-pa.

Author's Note

"Mayo!" That is the traditional greeting of Koi's people, the vast Batetela tribe of Central Africa. Its 70,000-mile expanse stretches from deep jungle, alive with wild game, to elevated grasslands, home to lions, leopards, and elephants.

I found the Batetelans to be a proud, intelligent people, friendly yet reserved, both rich in ancient traditions yet opening more and more to modern ways. Like Koi, they are learning to cope with relatives who have to live away in order to earn a living. Yet their folklore and customs are

55

proudly cherished—and handed down—from generation to generation. For instance, by the age of twelve, Batetelan boys and girls are allowed to build their own huts, separate from their parents' dwelling, yet nearby. Here they live until they marry or go to find work in the city.

The time I spent among the Batetelans was one of discovery and respect. They value their children, try to keep peace in their villages, and share generously with their neighbors. Despite the rich soil and wild game, daily life is hard and demands lots of work. Yet they always find time to gather as a family and tell of the great hunts and mighty exploits of old warriors such as Sankuru.

Africa, though, is changing, and the important Batetelans know that their future lies in education. Every parent wants this for his son and daughter. But what about the days of leopard-stalking and python-conquering? They are still just a quiet, dreamy thought away for the young Batetelans of Central Africa.

Now I give you the wish every Batetelan offers to his friend: *"Kutshu la wolu . . ."* (live in strength).

Enjoy More Hyperion Chapter Books!

ALISON'S PUPPY

SPY IN THE SKY

SOLO GIRL

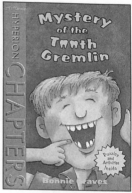

**MYSTERY OF
THE TOOTH GREMLIN**

**MY SISTER
THE SAUSAGE ROLL**

I HATE MY BEST

**ALISON'S FIERCE AND
UGLY HALLOWEEN**

SECONDHAND STAR

GRACE THE PIRATE

Hyperion Chapters

2nd Grade

Alison's Fierce and Ugly Halloween
Alison's Puppy
Alison's Wings
The Banana Split from Outer Space
Edwin and Emily
Emily at School
The Peanut Butter Gang
Scaredy Dog
Sweets & Treats: Dessert Poems

2nd/3rd Grade

The Best, Worst Day
Grace's Letter to Lincoln
I Hate My Best Friend
Jenius: The Amazing Guinea Pig
Jennifer, Too
The Missing Fossil Mystery
Mystery of the Tooth Gremlin
No Copycats Allowed!
No Room for Francie
Pony Trouble
Princess Josie's Pets
Secondhand Star
Solo Girl
Spoiled Rotten

3rd Grade

Behind the Couch
Christopher Davis's Best Year Yet
Eat!
Grace the Pirate
Koi's Python
The Kwanzaa Contest
The Lighthouse Mermaid
Mamá's Birthday Surprise
My Sister the Sausage Roll
Racetrack Robbery
Spy in the Sky
Third Grade Bullies